Beyond the Shallows

A Tidal Kiss Short

By Kristy Nicolle

First published by Kristy Nicolle, United Kingdom, February 2018

QUEENS OF FANTASY EDITION (1st Edition)
Published February 2018 by: Kristy Nicolle
Copyright © 2018 Kristy Nicolle

Edited by: Jaimie Cordall and Stephanie Farrant

Adult Paranormal/Fantasy Romance

The right of Kristy Nicolle to be identified as author of this Work has been asserted by her in accordance with sections 77 and 78 of the Copyright, Designs and Patents Act 1988.
All rights reserved. No part of this publication may be reproduced, stored in retrieval system, copied in any form or by any means, electronic, mechanical, photocopying, recording or otherwise transmitted without written permission from the publisher. You must not circulate this book in any format.

Disclaimer:
This ebook is written in U.K English by personal preference of the author. This is a work of fiction. Names, characters, businesses, places, events and incidents are either the products of the author's imagination or used in a fictitious manner. Any resemblance to actual persons, living or dead, or actual events is purely coincidental.

ISBN: 978-1-911395-13-3

www.kristynicolle.com

For Mrs. Helen Prochera,
Through trial by fire on the mountain of an island far out at sea, you and a small group of fictional boys formed me into the writer I am today.
I will never forget it, and I will forever be thankful to you most of all.

HAVEN'T READ THE TIDAL KISS TRILOGY?

START YOUR JOURNEY INTO THE OCCULTA MIRUM WITH…

BOOK 1- THE KISS THAT KILLED ME
BOOK 2- THE KISS THAT SAVED ME
BOOK 3- THE KISS THAT CHANGED ME

Prologue

ATARGATIS
ELYSIUM SHORES- THE HIGHER PLAINS

The plati-sun is descending toward the horizon which dances with dense bursts of magic froth, bouncing from the surface of the eternal seas that glisten, sapphire and pure beneath my knowing gaze. The silvery white rays of the orb, reflecting deep from within the platinum core of its spherical omniscience, fall through the diamond-tipped, stained glass of my bedroom window.

I inhale the air of the room and wish that breathing in and out deeply would give the same sense of relief as it had done when I'd been bound in mermaid form.

I hear his tread and my entire being vibrates at his closeness, at the fury which I know is coming. I know that we will continue the argument which raged this afternoon once he returns from the Olympian Council Chambers, but I'd hoped I'll at least be able to enjoy the plati-sunset first.

"You're home early," I grumble, feeling the seas, over which I rule, turning choppy as my temper threatens to build. I take another deep breath, to little effect, and turn to face my husband.

"Well, I'd think you would be surprised. Especially considering you're the reason I've been stuck in council most of this year. You can't just go around splitting mortal souls, Atargatis. We've talked about this before. Neither mortals nor Kindred need soulmates. I made the decree. You went against my wishes," he spits, his voice thunder and his eyes backlit with lightning forks. The chandelier of our bedroom, carved from the finest Mortarian crystal - a gift from my brother-in-law - tinkles slightly as Poseidon's fury mounts because my reply doesn't come in an immediate and apologetic flurry.

"I'm not apologising for what I did. I stand by it. The mer need soulmates. They need something to fight for." I blink slowly, once, then twice, watching his reaction as he sits down on the edge of our bed. His body crumples the powder blue silken sheets, woven with luciferin by the Fae to give them a comforting night time glow, for when the universe and my fights with my husband leave me restless and anxious as the moon rises above us.

"They have us to fight for. That's all they should need. Is immortal life not enough?" Poseidon asks, as I step gingerly forward, my toes connecting with the peppered gold and silver flakes embedded into the topaz of the floor. I slump onto the mattress as I reach my side of the bed, allowing the cloud of warm water vapour to hold me as I wonder how long we will have this same argument. Perhaps, in fact, we are doomed to repeat it for eternity.

"You have not been mortal… You have not felt the reliance on the senses that a mortal does, Poseidon. They need that which they can see, touch, taste… that which they can physically hold," I express, trying to make him understand.

"That's not the point of soulmates, Tara, you know that." He uses his pet name for me and I melt slightly. "You know that you could go anywhere in time and space and I would find you, I would love you, whether you were in this realm, this form, or any other. Your soul is what calls to me. With mortals, it is merely the immortal beauty you have bestowed to which they cling… they cannot see beyond that which is shallow." He turns, leaning down on our bedcloud which bends beneath his weight, compensating for his mightiness.

"Well… it's funny you should say that…" I give him a sly smile and his eyes turn suspicious, staring at me like a mortal would gaze upon one of their puzzles.

"Tara, what did you do?"

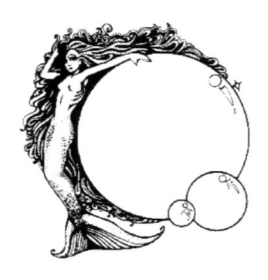

One

"*I wandered lonely as a cloud,
That floats on high o'er vales and hills.*"

Wordsworth- 'Daffodils' (1804)

OPHELIA
Blackpool, England, 1891

The open-top carriage trundles along the brick-paved street as we turn onto the seafront, jostling me as I continue to scan 'Daffodils' for the hundredth time this year. My eyes rise from the pages, yellowing at my hungry, private touch, to rest upon my two younger sisters, who are exchanging amused glances.

"What?" I demand of them, irritated, as I'm brought entirely too fast back to the present moment and my ears fill with the sound of gaudy, too happy songs and the clash of horse hooves against road.

"Nothing, we were just saying how funny it is that you're more interested in that silly old book than in the man who was just examining you as we passed." Ettolie giggles as Temperance shifts in her seat, her bustle rustling against the harsh leather upholstery. I sigh, wondering if the two of them ever have a thought that does not, in fact, involve a man.

"Oh, well, Wordsworth is more important than anyone you'll find around here," I reply, shrugging and feeling my hairpin come loose as we hit a hole in the road and the entire carriage tilts slightly to the left.

A long, dark ringlet of raven hair falls over my left shoulder from beneath my bonnet as I raise a hand to make sure my hat remains straight, not usually one for caring about my appearance but aware that reading in public as a woman is sin enough already.

"Well, I'd agree that this place has gone rather downhill since the working class started taking liberties with their new-fangled 'weekends', but you're going to end up a spinster," Temperance interjects, the contrast of her dark hair causing her pale skin to shine phantasmal, a sign of our class.

"And I shall be a happy one," I quip back at her. The pair turn horrified in their limited expressions and I roll my eyes.

"You shouldn't be so cavalier, Ophelia, you know how mother feels about your lack of interest in the opposite sex. It's why we're here!" Ettolie cries, fanning herself quicker with every passing word which falls from my defiant lips. I close my book, sighing at the fact I'm having to shut down the words of Mr. Wordsworth, and look her square in the face.

"Yes, yes, I know. For the Ozone. But you should know me well enough, sister, to know that I won't be married to just any boneheaded man with a pretty face and a title. I need… more," I whisper, feeling myself flush red at the subject of romance.

"What more is there?" Temperance demands, looking appalled as I shift in my seat, ready to set her straight. I am the eldest after all.

"Soul… my dear sister. There is soul. I need a man with soul, a man who can see past the glitter and glamour of a place like this and who understands the truth of feeling, of living, of love." I blink slowly, not breaking the intensity of my gaze, as Temperance goes to speak but then stops herself. Ettolie turns from staring out to sea and scowls.

"And what, oh divine prophet, Ophelia, is the truth of love? Hidden in those books you can't get your nose out of? Because, if so, I'd like to see it." She's snide now, crossing her ankles again and looking uncomfortable despite her bold tone.

"Well, I can tell you what it is not. It is not in a pair of cornflower blue eyes, or perfectly tamed hair. It is in the simplest of touches, the knowing glance betwixt you, in a man not only loving you, but loving you for who you are. For what makes you an individual, and certainly not for some rabid desire to marry the most beautiful, least educated trollop one might find simply for the pleasure of parading her about like some kind of prize pony at the Royal Norfolk Show!" I feel myself becoming angered by their lack of understanding, though I realise rather quickly that it's not just them to which I feel loathing, it is the entirety of my family. All except, of course, my Aunt Betty.

After my outburst, my two sisters look slightly taken aback as my chest rises and falls, constricted within my bodice, making me seem out of breath and overly exerted.

"Well, I still wouldn't marry someone ugly," Temperance huffs, partly defeated.

"Me neither," agrees Ettolie, continuing to fan herself and giving me the impression that she has not a single thought passing betwixt her ears. I'm sure though, if there is one, it's less reliable than the train between Peterborough and Lincoln, and that truly is something to be ashamed of.

We pass the rest of the journey in silence, looking out over the masses of people, dressed in their finery, parasols slung over their shoulders, protecting them from the dull rays of the sun, which peeks shyly from behind melancholy clouds. We pass Victoria pier, and my sisters clamber toward the left side of the carriage, squashing one another against the inside of the door to get a look at the entertainment that's available. I roll my eyes at them, wondering how they can find something so false, so put on, entertaining.

"We'll be arriving in only a few moments, M'lady," our chaperone informs us, turning back over one shoulder, whip in hand, and tipping his cap to me with the reigns of the horse still clutched in his other palm. I turn to face him, being seated facing the rear of the carriage, and nod, not feeling the need to reply or make conversation.

Proceeding along the seafront, we pass many houses, with others arriving just as we are. I am alarmed, however, at the level of crowding that has descended upon this once peaceful seaside town.

The paths are crammed with people, only inches from being hit by some handbag or parasol, bowler hats bobbing in a sea of expensive new clothes. The bodies within the mass are all but lost in a cacophony of overly fancy feathered headwear, too large bustles and long skirts. I watch the crowds teem, sweltering in the English summer heat - which foreign travellers would name as mild - and sigh, wondering if the sea air could possibly detach me from my longing for something greater, for something real.

The carriage pulls to a halt and I hear the horse exhale in a snort, stepping from one foot to the other as the driver gets down off his perch and opens the door. Of course, my sisters exit first, treading down into the masses of people and looking quite befuddled as to what to do next.

Hoisting up my skirt so it's hanging just above my ankles, I step down, feeling the carriage tilt beneath my weight, and move onto the pathway, shepherding the two lost lambs I call siblings across the street and into the garden of my Aunt Betty's seafront estate.

We approach the front door, painted in a dark navy blue with the number seventeen pinned to its surface in gold, but before Ettolie has a chance to raise a gloved hand and knock, the partition swings open, revealing the woman we have travelled so far to see.

"My goodness, such beautiful young women!" I hear the familiar, peppy tone of my favourite Aunt and practically push my two siblings over the threshold in an effort to get to her first.

"Ophelia!" She caresses my name with her tongue, making me feel like I had as a small girl, when she had come to visit. I used to love how she'd come from the seaside with tales both gruesome and incredible. She also brought books, brought poetry, and so I owe to her almost everything which I am.

"Aunt Betty. I have missed you," I gush, placing my arms around her shoulders, which are wrapped in a beaded white shawl, and holding her to my breast a moment before releasing her.

Our chaperone, Albert, begins to shuffle into the semi-detached seaside property with our luggage.

Stepping aside to let him through, I gaze upward and around at the hallway. It is, for certain, one of my favourite rooms I've ever frequented, bar the library near my home in London. The walls are a deep jade, with waterlilies painted, mural style, upon the thick wallpaper. Dark woods and mahogany floors spill throughout the house, giving it an intimate feel, with numerous bookshelves, stacked with adventures, romance, and comedy, making this perhaps the perfect sanctuary away from my mother and her obsession with marriage.

"How is Uncle Howard?" I ask my Aunt, who looks to me with an exasperated glance to the ceiling.

"Oh, he's a writer, you know how they get. He's off galivanting with his family in America somewhere, trying to chisel his way through a writer's block stubborn as marble."

"Well, you did marry him," Ettolie interjects and my Aunt nods, her navy-blue skirt skimming the highly-polished wood of the floor as she turns to face my sister.

"I did, and for that I am glad. He is the one man in this world who understands me utterly. That doesn't mean, however, that I always should like him. You will learn this once you are married." Her eyes crease, the sentiment meant to be kind and full of wisdom, but Temperance and Ettolie get a look of affront instead, though they may unsuccessfully try to hide it, and I roll my eyes.

"Perhaps, Aunt, it is because he understands you so utterly that you do not always like him," I suggest, trying to break the tension, and she laughs, patting me on the shoulder with a proud look in her eye.

"Of that, child, I am sure," she chuckles, before adding, "What have you ladies got planned for this afternoon? I'll be sending Albert to accompany you out, if you wish to go, for it would not be proper for me to let you go totally wild around Blackpool, would it?" She looks between us, and where Ettolie and Temperance nod with half sullen faces, I smile. One of the reasons my Aunt is my favourite family member is because she's so laid back. Albert is no more a strict chaperone than I am a bride, but my Aunt understands the need to placate those who put stock in appearance and etiquette over pleasure.

"I want to go and get a penny lick," Ettolie announces and I feel my heart sink. I was rather hoping that I could spend my entire stay between the stacks in my Uncle's library upstairs.

"I want to go and see the seaside entertainers," Temperance adds, jostling atop the balls of her feet so her ringlets bounce beside her ears. Both my sisters lack subtlety, yet another thing we don't have in common.

"What about you, Ophelia?" My Aunt looks to me and I shift, uncomfortable, though you wouldn't know it as I keep my change in position slight and my face delicate.

"I'm currently re-reading Wordsworth actually..." I remark and my Aunt smiles, though my sisters both sigh a little too loudly.

"Well, in your mother's letter she informed me the doctor has prescribed you with Ozone and plenty of it. You should accompany your sisters," she expresses, though behind her eye a twinkle lets me know she is only saying this to appease my sisters.

"You should all go upstairs and change into your finery, I'm sure you'll need to refresh yourselves after the train journey here. You'll want to leave soon, before the sun gets too low." She gestures to the steep incline of the mahogany staircase which climbs the left side of the hall. Dotted on the wall are many silhouettes of me and my sisters as we have grown, and some of Howard and his wife, too. Considering my Aunt has no children, she treats us like her own, and sometimes I find myself, however guiltily, wishing I was hers.

My sisters take their leave, climbing the stairs and moving to their usual twin room, where I have no doubt they will begin gossiping about my oddness almost immediately. My Aunt turns to me, gripping onto my wrist before I can take a single step.

"I have laid out a new book for you on your bed. More Wordsworth, I'm sure you'll enjoy it on the pier this afternoon." She winks at me and I nod, smiling at her, gracious. She truly understands me better than anyone I've ever met.

Turning toward the stairs, I place a hand atop her wrist in passing, hearing the door close finally as Albert brings in the last of our luggage and proceeds to follow me up to my room, bringing my cases with him. I tread carefully upon the wood floors, bringing my skirt upward once more so as not to catch the hem with my olive boots.

When I reach the landing, I rotate away from the balustrade and turn the ornate silver doorknob to the room I have occupied since I was a small child, every summer, when visiting my Aunt and Uncle, and step inside to the newly dusted room. The gas lamps, affixed to the walls seamlessly, gleam, and I move past the bottle green walls and over to the double bed as I take in the room and the nostalgia it always brings me, sending me back to a time where I had not been scared of marriage, scared of the future, but simply in awe of the power a dead man's words held over me.

Sitting down atop the silken bedspread of periwinkle blue, which has matching drapes, I see the book my Aunt spoke of, resting upon my pillow. I pick it up, relishing the smell as it falls open in my palms and the familiar blur of ink and parchment pulls me toward it like a magnet toward cast iron.

A knock on the door sounds, interrupting me and Mr Wordsworth once more, and I walk to open it, allowing Albert through the doorway so he can place my luggage on the blanket box at the end of the ornate four-poster. I sigh, hearing my sisters' giggles, as Albert proceeds out of the room, and go about unpacking my cases, knowing I need to redress.

Hauling the case upon the top of the bed, I unclip both clasps and raise the worn lid of the old leather luggage. As I examine the contents within, my eyes widen, and I notice that everything is new. New corsets, undergarments, bonnets, a floor length tailored overcoat, dresses and a pair of deep, bottle green heeled boots which close at the side with multiple mint green buttons. My mother's intentions for this trip were obviously more seeded in marriage than my health, which I realise now as she's only allowed me to bring one book with me, obviously forgetting the fact that her sister remains an avid collector.

I turn to the floor-length mirror as I shed the unnecessary and completely decadent garments in which I've travelled, starting with my bonnet. I often envy men, in their trousers and high boots, perfect for trekking, for running and exerting oneself over nature.

As I redress as quickly as I can, I take a moment to be glad that I'm alone. I loathe dressing at home, where my mother watches me like a hawk from corset to overcoat, judging the skew of every line and the stitch of every layer.

I stand, looking into my own silvery eyes before admiring the new clothes, which despite the fact I'm not one for fashion or aesthetics, I cannot deny compliment my complexion. With a bodice of dim teal lace, and a skirt which elongates my already tall form with layers of jade silks and satins. The bustle, which the women in London are slowly abandoning, sits on the back of my hips, ruffled in a colour reminding me of a deep marsh, or perhaps the ocean. Placing the thin bottle green overcoat over my dress and then adorning my head with a black, wide brimmed hat decorated with long olive feathers, I let my long ringlets fall down my spine, obscuring the high neckline of the gown as I adjourn across the room and pick up my new book.

"Ophelia, are you ready yet?" I hear the impatient tones of Ettolie travelling through the wood of my door and so quickly grab a black parasol from the bottom of my suitcase before yanking the door open and watching her startle. I giggle to myself at her too delicate sensibilities as I rush past her and down the staircase, where the third step from the bottom gives a familiar creak.

"Wait... is that a new coat?" I hear Temperance call from over the balustrade, looking down at me from above like a hawk.

"Yes," I reply, not looking up to her and proceeding through to the sitting room where my Aunt is sat, book in hand, half-moon spectacles resting on her nose. She hears me approach and smiles to herself.

"Your mother mentioned she was sending you with new attire. One would guess she is trying to attract a suitable husband." She doesn't look up, simply turning the page of the book she's reading and continuing to immerse herself.

"Yes, one would guess." I cock an eyebrow and Aunt Betty inhales deeply.

"Albert! My nieces are ready to leave." With this deafening decree, I hear the scuffle of shoes as my sisters descend the stairs and I turn, book and parasol in hand, treading delicately toward the hall.

I round the corner, having moved full circle throughout the house. I see the envious gazes of Ettolie and Temperance, who are dressed in last summer's fashions, but ignore them, stepping through the door - which Albert opened - and into the afternoon heat. The cry of gulls hits me, as does a stiff breeze, which robs the sun of its heat as we clamber once more into the open-top carriage and turn in the street, returning to where we had passed not an hour ago.

Upon the pavement once more, I feel myself not unlike I imagine a sardine feels in a jar. People are shoulder to shoulder, brim to brim, as they walk towards the jutting wooden outcrop, I'm sure for the afternoon entertainment. I watch bottlers on the side of the pier, ready to descend upon those who choose to watch the latest performance of H. Flockton Foster, hungry for spare halfpennies.

"Look, they're selling penny licks right over there! At the pier entrance." Temperance points, tapping Ettolie on the shoulder with so much enthusiasm that I fear she might push her over. I put up my parasol, careful not to injure anyone behind me, and follow them over to the line, passing men selling foxtails, visits to palmistry booths, and tickets to see two-headed mermaids in tanks, just down the promenade.

As we walk to the line for a penny lick, I turn, letting my eyes settle on the construction of what they're calling Blackpool Tower. Rising into the sky in jagged, metal monstrosity I feel my heart sink. It is not natural, or beautiful. It is not adding to the mysticism of the sea of which Wordsworth once wrote but instead taking away from it as it is erected, a gaudy beacon of cheap laughs and a human desire to prove we can do it better. I look down at the book in my gloved hand, feeling the weight of it, and wondering if the days of which the romantics had written are all but extinct now. I wish I'd been born earlier, if only I could've seen daffodils like Wordsworth, rather than being doomed to the inescapable blackness that is London smog.

"Nearly there!" Ettolie claps her white gloved hands together, like a small child in line for mint humbugs, as the line shifts so there is only one person in front of us, and I sigh, bored already. This afternoon is most certainly going to be torturous.

The woman before us is served and Ettolie and Temperance both lurch forward, pulling out their purses from their overcoat pockets and handing over one penny each. If you ask me it's an utter swindle, but who am I to deny them their happiness?

"Don't you want one, Ophelia?" Temperance turns to me, a tiny glass cup with a scoop of vanilla ice cream atop its tiny divoted surface, clutched in her silk clad fingers.

"Oh, no thank you. Too sweet for my tastes," I object, smiling at the server as he hands Ettolie the same glass cup.

Twizzling my black lace parasol, I follow the girls as they pull into the side of Victoria pier's grand entrance, looking out to sea as the waves froth upon the shore only metres beneath our feet. I watch the two girls as they take a single lick, devouring the entire delicacy in but moments, smiling, smacking their lips together, and then turning to return the glass cups to the stall from whence they came.

"Come on, let's go and get some seats for the three o'clock show," Temperance demands, pulling Ettolie behind her. The two of them make their way through the crowds, a bright plight of peaches and cream in their year-old fashions, and I trail behind, catching Albert watching us from afar.

"Ophelia, come on!" Ettolie calls over her shoulder, and I do as she demands, picking up my pace. We reach the theatre and I'm out of breath, the new corset pinching around my waist with an iron grasp tighter than what I'm used to.

"We're going to be late!" Temperance scowls at me and I sigh.

"You two go and get seats, I'm going to find somewhere to sit and read," I announce and they both look horrified, yet somehow unsurprised.

"You'll be lucky to get a seat on the safety rail with this crowd," Ettolie huffs, exasperated by my lack of enthusiasm for utter drivel, and I shake my head.

"I'll manage," I reply, turning from them and moving to the edge of the pier, to get a better view of my surroundings.

Seeing my sisters disappear into the crowd of pleasure-seeking tourists, I realise that Ettolie is not wrong about the seating. There is nothing, anywhere. Sighing, I decide that her comment about the safety rail might not be lost on me as I do something quite unladylike and climb atop it, perching myself and using my parasol to both shield my book from the weak sunlight and balance out the weight of my bustle.

Opening my book, I find balancing easier than I had intended, and am for once grateful for my mother's constant berating of my posture.

Slipping my new boot behind the middle bar of the construct, I flip through the pages, my fingers caressing the spine, realising that this might be the only collection of Wordsworth's I haven't yet read.

I feel the pull to the words, the excitement building in my chest at the inkling of new experience through the eyes of a man who knows how to feel, knows how to express and cut through all the unimportant icing on the cake of life; a man of substance.

As I'm staring down at the pages, ready to begin, a gust of wind suddenly picks up unexpectedly, though not so entirely for England, I suppose.

It lifts my parasol, averting my gaze out onto the choppy waters of the sea. It might be June, but they look tumultuous, and I find myself suddenly transfixed as something catches my eye, a glint of liquid gold among the waves, and I lean back to get a better glance.

Another gust of wind comes in quick succession, this one causing me to fall backward, the weight of my bustle leaving me utterly helpless, and over the edge of the rail.

I hear gasps from above, people staring over the ledge as I find myself, not panicking, but gazing, dazed, up at the sky whilst I fall, taking in its silver clouds, gilded with a golden light which feels somewhat familiar.

As I'm realising that this adrenaline is perhaps what I've been missing all along, and what has inspired so many poets before me, I crash into the salty froth of the Atlantic Ocean, my corset robbing me of my breath and causing me to fall into darkness shortly after.

Two

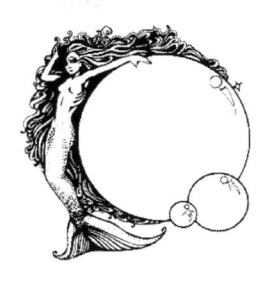

"The mighty Being is awake, and doth with his eternal motion make, a sound like thunder- everlastingly."
Wordsworth- 'It is a Beauteous Evening' (1802)

Air, like fire, burns its way into my lungs as I expel salt water like it is the devil and I a repentant. I sputter, my vision cloudy as golden eyes burn into mine. My paper-thin eyelids close, unable to stand the sting of the water, and when they open again reveal only darkness, interspersed with parallel lines of blinding light.

I am lying beneath the pier, washed up; though how I got here, how I am alive, I honestly cannot say.

"Miss! Miss!" I hear Albert's terrified voice growing closer as my head rests against the ground below and the world above spins, the lines of light forming kaleidoscopic whirls.

I feel myself bare, a chill running rampant through me, and lean up, looking down upon myself and becoming wide-eyed and horrified. My coat, dress, and corset have been savagely ripped asunder, my breasts spilling out of my undergarment which is soaked right through.

Alarmed, I cover myself, scouring my surroundings for any sign of my missing clothing but finding them empty. I feel something warm, heavy, and smelling of hay come around my shoulder as Albert wraps me in a blanket which I'm sure has also been used by a horse at some point, but cannot find the will to care as he picks me up in his unexpectedly large arms like a baby. He carries me, hair sodden and falling heavy from my head like rat's tails, back to the carriage, where the pathway is lined by onlookers, who cannot help but stop and stare at the silly girl who fell into the sea whilst reading poetry. I sigh, my mother is most definitely going to hear about this, and I suppose this also ruins my chances of finding a husband on this trip, not that I care.

"Alright, Miss. Just hold on tight, I'll have you home in no time." Albert gives me a kind smile, bowing his head to me with two fingers rested on the tip of his bowler hat. I warm to him in this moment, mainly because even though I'm sodden, half naked and cold, he's still treating me with the respect any regular person deserves.

"Thank you." I shiver, the chill making a desperate clutch at my bones as my teeth begin to chatter. Pulling away from the curb, I look out past the pier, past the masses of curious, judgemental faces and let my eyes rest upon the heaving vastness of unbroken blue. I'm searching for something, the same thing that had gotten me into this predicament: a flash of gold, of something real.

I sigh out, seeing nothing and letting another shudder claim me as I pull the horse's blanket more tightly around myself, abandoning my search and keeping my eyes on the road ahead.

"Wait, what about my sisters?" I ask Albert, who turns after giving his favourite whip a crack against the horse's rear.

"Fear not, Miss, I'll be back to chaperonin' once I've got you in the warm." He smiles, his crooked teeth sheening a light mocha in the now bright sun. This bright light, however, does nothing to warm me, and as we pull up once more to the front of my Aunt Betty's seafront property, I wince as the cold, heavy mass of my skirt sticks around my legs and my new boots squelch underfoot. Albert opens the door as I raise a soggy, gloved hand to knock, not sure why I'm embracing proper etiquette in a time like this, but beginning to become so tired I don't care.

"Back so soon?" I hear my Aunt's tone ring throughout the hallway, too loud, as the room begins to spin. "Oh, my Lord!" I hear her cry at the sight of me, bedraggled and unkempt, dripping all over her pristine mahogany floors.

"She might o' fell off the pier," Albert explains, flushing red as a new-born baby that's just been smacked across the behind.

"Might have fallen off the pier? Did she, or did she not, actually fall off the pier, Albert!? This is no time for flimsy discrepancies, on account of you fearing losing your employment." My Aunt crosses her arms, faux furious, as I stand, shivering under a horse's blanket.

"She did, Ma'am. Yes. She did fall off o' the pier." He continues to look shamefaced as my Aunt's wrath builds into a flurry of action.

"Come on! We don't want you to catch your death now, do we?" She doesn't look amused, her black hair, speckled through with grey, falling loose from her bun in the cacophony of her flapping arms as she shoos me up the stairs. As I climb the staircase, my feet sodden and pruning in my shoes, the third step from the bottom gives a familiar creak and I realise that her rage is probably more aimed at the fact my mother will be hearing about this, than the fact I've actually fallen off a pier.

"Ophelia, what happened?" she asks me once we're alone in my room. She takes the blanket from me, stripping me of any accumulated warmth and moves to light the fire. I begin to remove my sodden clothes, not sure of what to say.

"I... I don't know. I was sat on the safety rail, reading that book you gave me... The wind, it caught my parasol..." I begin, stuttering, realising that the book went in the water right along with me. It's gone. Lost.

At this notion, of those beautiful and real words swept away with the outgoing tide, I want to cry.

"You sat on the safety rail?" She looks incredulous, a glisten in her eye.

"Yes, there wasn't anywhere to sit. It's busy out there; we were shoulder to shoulder all the way down the pier. You should've seen it," I express and she nods.

"Yes, Blackpool is becoming worse, and by that, I mean busier, every year," she mumbles under her breath and stokes the fireplace with a cast iron poker, her face becoming aged as the flames play games of shadow with the deepening wrinkles upon her skin.

Having stripped down to my undergarments and nothing more, my Aunt fetches me a nightgown and orders me to bed.

"You look a funny shade of green, child. I think you best rest. Don't want you to miss out on the sea air for the rest of your stay, do we?" she asks rhetorically as I climb under the familiar, white, starched sheets of the four-poster bed. I watch then as she moves to collect up my wet clothes from the floor, smiling at me.

"I think I've had quite enough of the sea for now," I muse in an exhausted whisper, feeling the heat spreading from the fireplace, intoxicating to my body and making my chilled muscles relax. Today has been strenuous. The train, my sisters' constant twaddle, followed by the crowds of the pier and then the icy waters of the Atlantic. It's more than I'm used to certainly, for my days consist mostly of listening to my mother talk on the importance of courting, and reading when I can find a place to hide for some peace.

Thinking of liquid gold, my eyelids droop and I fall into a deep, but not entirely peaceful, sleep.

Crushed, bottle green velvet envelops me like a blanket, curling around my limbs and causing me to exhale a moan. The cry escapes my lips and flies up into the atmosphere, twisting like smoke, powered in flight only by the desire coursing through my flesh. My form shudders, tingling, coming alive at the soft clutch of the fabric, which cradles me, loving me, holding me, rippling into scales. In a moment of utter transformative power, the velvet fades once again, this time to flesh and back again, folding itself into shapes, into a man no less, who holds me close to his fast beating heart, as though I am a part of him, too.

I look upward, floating, hovering in a sea of tranquillity, and his oxymoronic stare takes hold of me, pulling me from this fantasy and into what's real. It drags me into pain and lust, love and hate, via the currents of two golden rivers, the rushing waters of which are unmistakable, and with depths quite beyond that which I am able to fathom.

Maintaining eye contact with this velvet-made man, we fall through the sky, the sun blazing down from a limitless cruel black, as though it is reflecting the dark sea beneath my feet. I watch as we fall before the sun, and a needle and thread form from nearby clouds, stitching together the one who holds me, part flesh, part fabric, like an ugly ragdoll of reality with two golden buttons for eyes that burn into my very soul. He is beautiful, despite the fact others might view him as unutterably hideous. He is without aesthetic safeguarding, without icing so to speak. He is real. He is substance.

Reaching the ocean, a pier appears beneath my feet, supporting me as he lets go and floats away from me on the tide. I rush forth,

my body bare and cold without him as the pier rises like a mountain from the sea, leaning over the railing of the construct and crying out to the endless mercilessness of the waves.
Bring him back. Please. Bring him back.

I wake in a cold perspiration, determined to sleep no more, starting and sitting bolt upright like a shoot in early spring, straight toward the sun in a desperate frenzy to taste life.

Except now, I realise, the sun is absent and the fire in the hearth has long since extinguished, as the moon hovers, quite risen, outside my window. My heart is hammering in my chest, desperate for more, for the velvet man. For how can anything compare to such a decadent soul?

I swing my legs out of the side of the bed, shedding the heavy blanket cocoon, recovered entirely from my fall this afternoon.

What time is it?

A ticking clock on the wall next to the bed informs me that it is a few minutes to midnight, and so I take a self-igniting gas lamp in my palm, place my dressing coat over my shoulders and slip my still damp boots, which sit beside the dark fireplace, on my pale feet, unable to stay in the confines of the room a single moment longer.

I turn the doorknob, careful to be as quiet as possible as I stumble onto the landing in the dark. I tread lightly down each step of the staircase, careful to make sure my lamp doesn't hit the balustrade and my boots do not scuffle upon the mahogany floorboards. When I reach the third step from the bottom, I move without thinking, cringing as my foot comes down on the stair.

As a groan emits, midnight falls, and the chiming of many tightly wound grandfather clocks ring out through the house, masking the sound of my rookie error. As the chimes toll on, climbing gradually to the great tonal height of twelve, I scramble for the door, hoisting my nightdress just above my ankles and ensuring I am out of the front garden before the final bell rings out into the night.

Standing on the path, I realise that I might have suffered a mild bout of insanity during my fall this afternoon, as I'm standing in my nightclothes in the middle of the night on the seafront, but then, I realise.

How marvellous this is. To be free of expectation and demand under the shadow of the night and the moon's full light. I muse, poetic in spirit as I step across the deserted road.

The night is quiet, all except for the flickering of lamps long since lit by gas-lighters and the crashing of waves against the sodden shore. Beyond the street, I let my feet find the sand dunes, which drop dramatically down to the shore in abrupt lines of chalky descent. Blades of grass, sparse yet persistent, poke through the sand and catch against the soft flesh of my ankles as I make my way toward a path, carved so that tourists may take leisurely to the sand without ruffling their feathers.

As I descend, the wind whips through my hair, and as I reach sea level, I find myself gazing upon the unmistakable but dim outline of Victoria Pier. It calls to me, whether it be the trauma of my fall, hysteria, or the dream from which I've so suddenly awakened with wanderlust.

I take step after careful step along the shoreline, the waves calling to me on a level I cannot describe except to call sublime. Is this what Wordsworth felt when he looked upon it and wrote 'By the Sea'? Is this feeling of immense unworthiness, of being so utterly dwarfed by forces beyond mortal comprehension what led him to bleed upon parchment?

As I near the pier, I catch sight of something, a shadow, flitting between supporting beams which are encrusting with molluscs and crustaceans.

"Who's there?" I call out, wondering if this is in fact the right action to take. I am a woman, unchaperoned and out in the middle of the night in my bedclothes. If I am caught by a spiteful individual, this may be enough to have me committed. I am not proper, but then this is far from surprising, as the only thing which keeps me this way during daylight hours is the duty I feel toward my family's reputation.

I take a single step forward, my face cast in shadow under the light of the very almost full moon. Something comes flying from the shadow, thrown by the figure hiding beyond the wooden stilts of the pier. It lands at my feet, causing an up spray of sand to cover my boots. I look down at it, a saturated mass of pulp and ink which was once some of the greatest human sentiment ever recorded, the book lies at my feet.

"Where did you get this?" I call out into the dark, feeling my heartbeat quicken as I bend down to take the ruined artefact in hand. Was this who had pulled me ashore this afternoon?

"You dropped it, when you fell." The voice is gruff as it echoes out from the shadow, and I feel the shift in his presence as he moves from behind one pillar to another. I catch his silhouette briefly, damnably human in general outline, but with alarmingly webbed hands and feet. I gasp a little, feeling my breath quicken beneath the flimsy white cotton of my nightgown as I take a pace backward, almost tripping over my skirt as I do so.

"Did... Did you save me?" I ask, my voice coming in shallow, fleeting wisps.

"That best portion of a good man's life, his little, nameless, unremembered acts of kindness and of love." The quote comes from the darkness and I inhale sharply, the words so familiar they could be from my own lips.

"You... you know Wordsworth?" I know I must sound terribly uppity, as the surprise in my voice comes out in a high-pitched squeak.

"Yes." The reply seeps from the darkness, and the sound of sea spray drips from the wood of the pier overhead and down to the damp sand below.

"Come forth into the light of things." I ask this of him, once again using the words of the wisest person I know to articulate myself, worrying that my own words are less than adequate. This man might be disfigured - a freak even - but he saved my life and I should thank him for that.

"No. I cannot," his reply comes, pained and full of fear. My heart palpitates beneath my breast, longing to see his face as curiosity overtakes me.

"I will not judge you. With an eye made quiet by the power of harmony, and the deep power of joy, we see into the life of things." I quote the poet we both know once more and observe as the figure hesitates, lurking in the dark even still, but gradually moving forth into the dim light of the moon.

I raise my gas lamp to his face for a more detailed examination, but upon illumination, my breath catches in my throat. His grotesqueness penetrates my vision and possesses my mind so completely, that as I stand, wind slamming into me barely noticed, I don't know what to say.

He was a man, once, I think... but his skin now is marred with a hundred scars, some stitched back together, and others left to heal on their own from where some kind of hook has torn his cheeks asunder. This, however, isn't his most remarkable plague, as his flesh ripples from milky white to deep, repugnant, green. The scales aren't even consistent, not giving him the mercy of being his entirety, but rather patchwork across his form, which stands, topless, before me.

Is this what makes me speechless? Momentarily perhaps, but soon it is his eyes, their familiar liquid gold, which to some may become unnerving as they are almost too bright, too piscatorial and bulging from his face. I think that he may have been quite handsome once, too, his forehead being broad and brow low hanging, jaw firm and his body lean, but it is almost impossible to tell now due to his deformities. I look down to his hands and bare feet, to where his appendages are gloved in the same mouldy looking scales, webbing his limbs into a solid lump of ungodly flesh, binding him to the water and whatever lies in its most terrifying darkness.

Suddenly, I realise I may have been silent for far too long as his eyes become sad, the depth of their emotional capacity evident to me immediately when he moves to turn away. Reaching out without thought, acting purely on instinct, I grab his wrist, laying my flesh upon the soft velvet of his, and stop him in his tracks.

"Thank you for saving me," I whisper, looking into his eyes and not daring to blink. He is not beautiful, but neither are some of the most fascinating natural phenomena. Not everything has to be beautiful to be worth one's time.

"You're welcome. I couldn't let you drown. I've been watching you, sitting, reading. I hoped it was poetry. I love the romantics." His voice is gruff, almost as though I'm the first person he's spoken to in years.

"Can I ask... what's your name? I'm Ophelia." I hold out a hand, bare flesh vulnerable to him as I'm without my gloves. He examines me, cocking his head as mid-length black locks fall over his bare shoulder.

"I'm... well, you may call me Dagon," he coughs, taking my hand and shaking it with his own green, scale-gloved palm, unsure of what to do. I do not flinch at his irregular touch, but look up at him, trying to see the man behind the plague of scales, the face that had once been, and smile.

"Dagon. That's pretty," I express, and he blinks a few times, confused.

"Pretty isn't a word one would ever associate with a creature such as myself, but you are, nonetheless, sweet for saying so." His lips part, showing a set of crooked teeth, which remain intact despite the trauma to his face. I reach up, cautious as my palm shakes with anticipation, wanting to touch him desperately despite knowing better.

"What happened to you?" I ask, unable to keep myself silent about the obvious any longer, but then realising that we are only strangers. My hand stills in its course toward his flesh as he pulls away. "Of course, you don't have to tell me if you feel it improper." I avert my gaze, feeling inferior to his massive gait. It's not like me, feeling this way when pitted against a man, but there's something about him that makes me timid, some sublimity that gives the impression he is older than the pier we're stood beneath.

"I am cursed, by Poseidon," he murmurs, though I'm listening so intensely that even his shame cannot diminish the weight of his confession.

"What quarrel does the God of the sea have with you?" I query him, wondering what a single man could do that would be so awful as to warrant such a punishment.

"His beloved, Atargatis, bound in maiden form, became caught in my net… many years ago when I worked as a mortal fisherman. I reeled her in and she turned to sand before my very eyes. I could not avert my gaze from her unearthly beauty as she burned up in the sunlight. That was where my eternal penance began." He cannot look me in the eyes as he confesses to this sin, looking out over the ocean in an attempt to remain distant from me.

"You looked at her? That's all?" I ask him, my mouth popping open. He turns back to me, eyes wide, and nods.

"Poseidon said that I was not worthy of her beauty, and for releasing her from his scaled prison that I was not worthy of love at all, for I had caused his relationship harm. So, I woke up the next day like this. I was chased from my village, and I've been fleeing my fate ever since," he expresses, depressed as he sighs, and I feel my heartstrings pluck a melancholy tune for his solitude.

"How old are you?" I enquire, wondering if I'm still dreaming.

"Older than you. Five hundred or so? I've lost count," he admits, placing his hands in the pockets of his dress trousers and kicking the sand absentmindedly with one webbed foot.

"The things you must have seen…" I gasp, thinking about what it must entail to live for so many eons.

"Not so. I cannot walk among men. Nor can I find anyone like me in the oceans. In fact, the closest thing to me is the Kindred of Atargatis herself, the mer, and I'm currently being hunted by them," he scowls, clearly aggravated, and I cock my head.

"Mermaids? Mermen? They're… real?" I gawp, and he chuckles.

"For someone who didn't think twice at resting their eyes upon me, you seem awfully surprised." He shakes his head, his face transformed as he looks upon me with affection. I blush, this becoming only too obvious against my pale flesh, I'm sure.

"Yes, as far as I can tell, Atargatis' presence here caused demons to become attracted to this dimension, she needed someone to defend the seas in her stead, so created the mer to do her bidding," he explains, and I nod slowly, taking it in. My heart is racing with many questions blooming from each single beat, but my head is telling me to slow down and listen, knowing I can muse the probability of this later.

"I see."

"I know it is hardly likely you will believe any of this, after all, tomorrow you will wake up and convince yourself I am a dream and go back to your hunt for a husband, I'm sure." He smiles at me, the sentiment supposedly kind, but for some reason it awakens my temper, pushed down for so long and now returning to the surface of my conscious.

"What makes you think I need a husband?" I ask him, placing my hand, still clutching the drenched works of Wordsworth, on my hip.

"Don't all women?" He cocks a scaled eyebrow at me and his eyes sheen, illuminating the dark with their persistent metallic canary.

"I need nothing more than literature and a quiet place in which to consume it, Sir." I address him with respect, a trickle of fear still present in the back of my mind despite the fact that he's been nothing but genteel.

"A woman after my own shrivelled heart," he muses, his gaze becoming playful.

"Shrivelled? How so?" I demand of him, interested in his physical anatomy.

"How could anyone ever love me? You look upon me and you do not know what I have done, the men I have drowned in the stead of my own survival. I am a monster, Ophelia. The fact that you cannot see it makes me only more certain of your naivety, of your need for guidance, your need for marriage and security in this world. You know not of the cruelty of man. Not really." His condemnation tempts my fury further and I stamp my foot beneath my nightdress.

"How dare you? How dare you judge me by my appearance. I may seem meek, but I have struggled. A woman with a brain in her skull, a woman who desires adventure, who desires what is real. Who desires more than just some… some… happily ever after! Is not one immune to adversity, I assure you," I exclaim, finding myself yelling now as Dagon's expression turns surprised and he actually takes a step back from me. My knuckles are white as I look down and find my fists clenched around the handle of my lamp and spine of the book, my furiousness exerting itself over material objects, but giving me little relief from the storm I feel raging within my chest.

"Alright, I'm sorry. I shouldn't have assumed," he stutters.

"No. You shouldn't," I condemn him, scowling and feeling my brows knit together. His eyes turn hopeful a moment and he continues to gaze at me.

"It's a shame that book got so badly damaged… I was hoping to have something to read while I wait for this hunter to move on and leave me in peace." He sighs, changing the subject.

"Well, you did save my life. I can bring you another if you'd like," I offer, feeling bad for yelling at him almost immediately, and wondering why I care what he thinks so badly.

"You would do that… and stay?" he asks. I open my mouth to refuse, unsure what he means, before he elaborates by saying, "I'd like to discuss the poems with you… it's not easy to find someone versed in the romantics out there." He gestures to the waves, which lap, calmer now, against the damp sand of the shoreline and I blink once, twice, three times, thinking on what things must be like for him. Perhaps, just perhaps, his suffering has made his soul rich, made it decadent and substantial enough for me to partner with my own, if only for a night.

"Very well," I agree, and he looks surprised.

"You're certain?" he asks me, and I nod, unsure but not wanting to betray my uncertainty to him as he seems more fragile than he appears in ego.

"I am. I'll meet you here tomorrow night, at dusk." I set the time and date, knowing that it might be difficult to steal away, but hoping I can wander off after a late afternoon on the promenade unnoticed.

"I cannot wait, Ophelia. Thank you." He takes my bare skin in his palm, more confident now we have an engagement tomorrow night, and raises my hand to his slightly flabby lips, where he plants a gentle kiss.

"Thank you… for what? It is you who saved me." I curtsey to him, though feeling a little embarrassed for I am still dressed in my night gown and dressing coat.

"For the very fact that you did not flinch at my touch," he whispers to me, and with that, he turns and disappears into the waves. I watch him as he goes, truly of the sea, but not entirely a monster, feeling my heart drifting away with him and the outgoing tide.

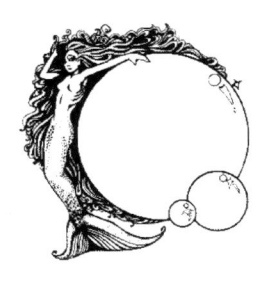

Three

> "Chains tie us down by land and sea;
> and wishes, vain as mine, may be
> all that's left to comfort thee."
>
> **Wordsworth- 'The Affliction of Margaret' (1807)**

"Did you have a nice time out, alone, in the early hours of this morning, Ophelia?" my aunt enquires, passing me a silver platter of butter and knife. I look down at my plate, ready to apply - with militant precision, I might add - the thick creamy spread to my toasted bread soldiers. Her question alarms me after a moment, as I register what she's just said, and my sisters' eyes rise from their plates to gape at me.

"I beg your pardon?" I reply, feigning innocence as she cocks her head at me, eyes tired from so many years of knowing all.

"Your boots are covered in fresh sand, Ophelia, and your tread is not as careful as you may believe. Do not treat me as an invalid, please." She raises her eyes from her busy hands, which work, peeling the shell from her soft-boiled egg in front of her, eyebrow raised with a look of utter condemnation plastered on her face.

"I needed some fresh air, Aunt, that is all. I woke up from a dream feeling quite off-colour," I explain in half-truth, knowing full well that which had crept into my mind last night was the strangest dream ever to befall me, but also knowing it was not the dream alone that had called me to the shore. It had been him.

"I see, and you didn't think it wise to wake Albert? A young woman, as free in spirit as she may be, should not be out of bed and walking the streets alone, Ophelia. Your mother would surely hang me up by my ankles if she knew you'd been out so late alone." She purses her lips together at the thought of her sister and I exhale heavily. I haven't been thinking about the fact that I'm under her charge for the duration of this stay. I may be in my mid-twenties, but I suppose I am unmarried, and therefore cursed to be thought of as an incapable child until I have one of my own.

"I apologise, Aunt. I was not thinking. I was quite rattled after my fall yesterday." I begin to dig into my breakfast of soft boiled egg, plunging the buttered soldiers into the rich yellow of the yolk's depths. My aunt sighs, smiling at me, though her eyes betray weariness even still.

"Well, even I cannot deny that the Ozone is helping already, your midnight jaunt seems to have done you the world of good. You look radiant this morning." The compliment falls on deaf ears as I catch my sister's watching me with amusement as the dark navy walls of the dining room almost fully absorb the morning sun. I wonder what they're staring at, but then realise that my skin is slightly glowing, a stark contrast to the rich, deep hues of my surroundings.

Breakfast passes in silence, and once the morning tea is sipped dry and the egg whites emptied from their shells, I climb the stairs back to my room to dress, feeling lighter than I have done in a while. During the morning meal, my mind has been wandering to Dagon, to his face, his tongue and how it caresses the words of Wordsworth so completely, as though they are as valuable to him as they have always been to me. I wonder, is it not possible that he might be available for more company than just one night? I am lonely, not in physical company, but in company with someone who has a similar love for words and the depth of emotion they can create from even the most mundane of things.

Pivoting toward my room before entering, I sigh loudly, realising that soon I'll be back in London, away from the sea, and so I guess it just is not meant to be.

"Did you just hear our sister sigh, Ettolie?" Temperance's voice creeps over my left shoulder and I rotate back, my slippers gripping the floorboard with adequate traction, and find them both, narrow eyed in the doorframe.

"I believe I did, Temperance," Ettolie replies, the lace frills on her nightgown vibrating with the excitement that is ebbing between them both.

"What do you two want?" I ask, placing one hand on my hip and raising one brow ever so slightly.

"Nothing, sister, we were just wondering what the *real* reason you went out gone the chime of midnight was," Temperance asks me, unabashed as her dark hair spills over her shoulders in loose curls. Her dark eyes sheen just like Ettolie's at the thought of scandal, but I merely shrug.

"I told you the real reason over eggs," I merely say, not wanting to share my unexpected closeness with a stranger with two of the most aesthetically obsessed people I know.

"Oh, come on, Ophelia. We know you better than that. You're glowing this morning. It was a man, wasn't it?" Ettolie suggests and I feel my cheeks flush - against my will - with colour as my entire body goes rigid and my skin heats.

"No…" I feel more embarrassed than I should, but it is not because of the sex of the companionship which I wish to engage in, it is because they're going to want me to describe him, and how can I possibly even begin?

"Oh, my Lord, it *is* a man!" they both say in unison, erupting into a fit of overly audacious giggles and slamming my bedroom door dramatically behind them, lurching across the threshold.

"No… I didn't say…" I stutter, and the two of them launch themselves - still dressed only in nightgowns and dressing coats - onto the unmade sheets of my four-poster bed, looking up at me as though I am God.

"Oh, do tell us, Ophelia. Please!" Ettolie whines, her feet jiggling in anticipation.

As Temperance's eyes narrow, scrutinising me, I realise that I'm not going to be able to silence them on this issue until I give them at least a small amount of information to salivate over.

"Alright, you caught me. I did meet a man last night, it was the one who saved me from drowning yesterday," I confess and the two of them take a synchronised and sharp inhale of breath.

"Oh wow, he saved you? It's meant to be!" Ettolie gushes and I roll my eyes.

"This isn't a romance novel, Ettolie. He was nice, we talked, that's all, we're meeting again this evening, to discuss poetry actually," I reveal, and she gets a confused look on her face, almost as though her brain is working so hard it's painful.

"He reads? As in, that ridiculous, pompous, twaddle that you read?" Temperance takes the words right out of our sister's mouth and I scowl, feeling my blood start to boil.

"One, William Wordsworth is without a doubt the greatest romantic poet, perhaps the greatest poet who ever lived. Two - which you may need to be reminded comes after the number one - not everyone is so entertained by penny lick ice cream and H. Flockton Foster, some of us have substance and, for that matter, refined taste!" I spit and the two of them grow wide-eyed.

"Wow. You must really like this poetry worshipper to be so defensive," Ettolie retorts, her face annoyingly un-phased by my insult of her intellect, if it does, in fact, actually exist.

"Whether I do or do not is none of your concern," I mutter and the two of them return to standing, their motions all too symmetrical.

"Well, we won't help you get ready then, if we're so stupid and it's *none of our concern.*" Temperance is snide in her tone, biting her bottom lip as she tries to hide a sly smile. They know I'm awful at doing my own hair, and after yesterday's bath in the Atlantic I am frightfully at the mercy of their expertise if I want to look presentable.

"You two are cruel," I sigh, realising that I am defeated.

"Oh, we know, so much so that there's a condition to our help," Ettolie announces, sidling over to me.

"Which is?" I ask them, feeling my heartbeat thudding dully in my chest at the prospect of being at the mercy of two such superficial beasts.

"We want to know what this man of yours looks like. All the details," Ettolie continues and Temperance's eyes gleam in triumph as I sigh, knowing that for the life of me, the truth of the matter they will most certainly never believe.

We stride along the prom after a day of constant examination by my two sisters, Albert trailing behind us more diligently than usual, which I'm sure is down to my little trip into the sea yesterday. We have just finished taking a late afternoon tea at the Imperial Hotel, courtesy of my Uncle Howard, who had arranged for the engagement as apology for not being around to receive us this visit. The sandwiches - cucumber, cheese and cress - were refreshing and did nicely alongside the piping hot china pot of Twinings earl grey, soothing my nerves at the prospect of tonight's meeting with Dagon. I feel anxious about laying my gaze upon his form, twisted and mangled with scales, once more, as I'm beginning to wonder how it was I had not passed out from fright last night. Any normal woman would have, any normal woman should have, but I for some reason had merely seen a person who was suffering, who was tormented down to his very soul. The look in his eyes still haunting me whenever I close my own, I sigh out, twizzling my parasol and taking the stroll at a leisurely pace as the crowds around us hurry home, wanting to be in before the sun sets, leaving the pier cold and uninviting. My goal, however, is to somehow persuade my sisters to lie about my whereabouts to my Aunt, and Albert, so I may go and meet Dagon alone.

"Oh look, Palmistry!" I hear Ettolie cry, breaking my internal monologue and causing me to turn my head to where she is pointing, my bonnet moving uncomfortably against the back of my neck as I strain to see. She is of course, correct and astute in her assessment of the gaudy looking tent, no doubt filled with trinkets paid for by the desperation of prior clients.

"Oh, I wish we could go. I'm out of money though!" Temperance complains, pulling out her black silken purse and staring hopefully into the depths for spare pennies. An idea occurs to me, hitting me when I need it most.

"If I pay for us to go and see the palm reader, will you help me get away to see my friend tonight?" I ask them as they both turn to me with surprised looks on their faces.

"That sounds fair. What do you want us to do?" Ettolie asks, grabbing my elbow and pulling me across the street, winding our way around carriages and past impatient horses as she puts an increased distance between us and the chaperone.

Once across the other side of the street, I frown, looking at my two siblings In their peach and lilac finery. The wide brims of their hats shield them from the sun and my parasol casts further shadow over their faces, but is yet unable to diminish the mischievous glint held captive behind their dark irises.

"Just tell Aunt I went for a stroll to get some more sea air and I'll be back soon. Tell her I wasn't feeling well, too hot... I don't know, anything. Just buy me some time," I express and the two of them look between themselves and then at me.

"Alright... but you are, you are being careful, aren't you, Ophelia?" Ettolie's eyes turn worried now and Temperance's mouth skews to the left slightly, displaying that she, too, is concerned.

"Yes, I'll be fine, I promise. You trust me, don't you?" I ask them and they both nod, though the look of uncertainty remains between them.

"We just, we know that we tease you, but you're a good sister. We love you, with our whole hearts. We want you to be careful." They both look at me sternly, my two younger sisters giving *me* a lecture.

"You could ruin your reputation... or worse," Temperance reminds me.

"I know, but I so rarely find someone with whom I have so much in common. I know you don't understand, you have one another... but I... I feel so lonely sometimes." This seems a rather open conversation to have in the middle of a crowded street, but it also feels kind of nice that they both care so deeply about me. With how they usually act you wouldn't know it.

"Alright, let us go and see what your future has in store," Ettolie announces, pulling me over to the tent which is set up, beachside, and adjacent to the crowded path.

"My future?" I exclaim, looking at her with an expression of horror plastered across my face.

"Well, of course. I already know what my future holds; a gorgeous husband with a manor house and several curly-haired babies." Ettolie states this as a matter of fact as she sweeps aside the threadbare plum curtain, which acts as a doorway, at the entrance to the tent and we step into the dim glow of several low burning candles, closing our lace parasols. Temperance bends low and enters behind us as I shoot her an uncomfortable glare over my shoulder.

"Good afternoon, ladies. Take a seat and Madame Lola will tell you all...." The gypsy with a rustling belt of coins and top too low cut for decency gestures, swirling her fingers which are adorned with many thick, crystal rings and pointing for us to be seated around the circular table which is covered in black velvet. The walls of the tent hold many trinkets, all of which I'm sure are fake, or have been procured only for this gimmick from which the gypsy makes her living, but instead of taking time to glance around at all of them, I sit as the woman suddenly grasps my gloved hands in hers.

"Oh... look at you, maiden of the Tidal Kiss. Aren't you so beautifully fractured..." she mutters, unnerving me entirely as she removes one of my gloves before I can say no and lays a weathered, calloused palm upon my own, turning it around in her hand.

As my sisters are seated either side of me, Madame Lola requests payment, which I hand to her, feeling foolish, before she goes back to examining the pale lines mapping my palm.

"Hmm.... Very interesting. Though I need not read your palm to know what fate has in store for you, Ophelia." She speaks my name and I look down to examine myself, and then left and right to my sisters. How exactly is it that she'd guessed my name? Is it some kind of tell in my appearance, or did she hear one of my sisters mention my name before we even entered the tent?

I smile graciously, not wanting to appear either rude or in awe of her so-called clairvoyance.

"What? What is it?" Ettolie asks, leaning forward and clapping her gloved palms together.

"Your sister is destined for the waves. Though... not in the most usual of senses. Her calling is a little more... monstrous than one would usually be matched with." Her words take me by surprise as I yank my hand from her grasp and snatch up my glove from the table.

"Ettolie, Temperance, we're leaving!" I snap, spinning on one heel and storming from the tent, my face flushing red with embarrassment and horror at the words which she has laid bare before me. How does she know about Dagon? Did she see us last night?

My heart begins to pound, and I feel my ribs bursting against the heavy binding of my corset. I put up my parasol, raising it above my head, and hear the disgruntled calls of my siblings, who emerge from the tent behind me and into the busy street.

"Ophelia, wait! What happened?" They both gush, demanding an explanation with wide and worried eyes, failing to mask their excitement at my dramatic exit.

"She is such a swindler... You two, you should know better than to fall for someone's... cheap tricks!" I burst, my first inclination being to dismiss the legitimacy of the gypsy all together.

"Sister, it is alright. I'm sure she meant nothing by it. She is only a fortune teller... Don't give it a second thought." Temperance lays a hand on my shoulder, equally as dramatic in her response as I had been in my exit. I turn to her, stood still in the midst of the street which is clearing of its usual heavy crowds.

"You two, hurry along now, go and find Albert. I must go and find a bookstore before the sun sets," I express, shooing them away and wondering why the words of Madame Lola had affected me so. Is it because she has described the person I feel so close to, after so little time, as a monster? Or is it because I'm not sure if she's wrong?

"Alright, be safe. We will be waiting to hear all about your adventure when you return home. Just try not to be too late. We don't want to have to listen to another breakfast rant." Ettolie nods to me as the two women turn and walk back up the street together, silhouetting against the low hanging sun as they approach our chaperone. I watch them explaining my wish to be alone to him, and he looks to me a moment, his expression concerned as well. I wave to him, a genteel and serene smile masking my utter terror at the night ahead as I spin on my heel and tread briskly down the promenade, wishing to disappear into the crowd, which seems never busy enough when one requires it, before he can question me any further.

I try to steady my breathing as I leave the tent and the fortune teller far behind me, searching for my favourite bookstore among the gaudy outlines of many trinket and souvenir stores. I find it right where I remember: between a curiosity shop and a pawnbroker. It stands, meek and worn in its signage, and yet holding stock of far more value than anything for miles from its dim lit front door. Treading back across the tram lines and between parked carriages, I make haste, aware that the store will soon be closing.

Entering, I quickly scour the stacks of shelves, running my fingers along the spines of many leather-bound volumes before finding a suitable collection of Wordsworth - my favourite in fact - and going to purchase it at the cash register.

Gripping the book in my gloved palm, I step out of the store into the dim light of sunset, and as I do so the shop owner turns the sign on the dim glass from *Open* to *Closed*.

I let my parasol swing down beside my left thigh, which rustles against the innermost layer of my overly fine gown. I had let my sister's dress me, and they had chosen well, putting me in another sea green dress, though this one is panelled with black lace and slims my figure even more than usual. I examine myself for lint or debris as I make my way back to the pier, where tired looking tourists are trundling back to their accommodation or the station, their fun dying with the very last light of the sun as it disappears behind the now deep hue of the horizon.

Making my way down the dunes of sand, slathered in hideous concrete, I make it to the edge of the beach, just as the sky turns to midnight blue.

My heart pounds as the minutes pass, and I wait, only the sound of waves lapping against the grain of the shore to keep me company. After around twenty minutes, I open the book and attempt to read, the full moon giving just enough glow to take in the words as my anxiety creeps, ever so slowly, to levels of higher and higher intensity within my chest.

Reading kills some time, but before long, I begin to realise that I've been jilted.

I sit, discouraged and feeling as though this is a sign that relationships with the opposite gender just aren't for me. Whilst I'm pondering this, it occurs to me that perhaps I had dreamed Dagon up to fulfil my own longing for company. Am I really that lonely?

In answer to my question, my name comes - a strangled cry from the shoreline, barely audible above the crashing of a wave.

"Ophelia!" The gruff caress of the word, coupled with the anguish behind it, causes me to lurch to my feet from where I've been sitting in the sand.

Hoisting up my skirt to just above the ankle, I hop across the sand to where the pier fully covers the shoreline beneath it.

I see him, a messy outline, a pile of flesh, washed up on the shore, flopping around as though he is now fully piscatorial.

"Dagon!" I exclaim, pulling my skirt even higher - beyond what is proper - and dashing across the sand and into the damp of where the sea meets the land.

"Ophelia..." He coughs, his face barely visible between the lack of moonlight and mess of scales which bury his pale features.

"What happened to you?!" I demand, looking down to his chest. His pectoral has been gauged by something sharp and his deep red blood - human blood - is spilling out in a gushing torrent, mixing in with the green of his scales, making him appear like a painter's palette unwashed.

"The hunter... he found me." I feel his reverence, his fear, in every word. Looking down into his eyes, some of their precious metallic sheen has diminished, almost as though the wick of his life's flame is burning out.

"It's alright... it's alright. We'll get help! We'll get... a doctor." My mind is racing, my heart running wild at the thought of the life leaving his face, of his soul becoming no more.

"Ophelia, you can't. They'll lock me up. Put me on show. No." His voice breaks at this final sentiment and I can see that this is a fear so deeply embedded within him that there's no way he has not had an experience which has marred him this way. I look around, to the sky, to the sea, for anything that can help him, save him, as the waves come up and drench me through, making me shudder.

"Get out of the way... girl." I hear the voice and the cold water is no longer what makes my flesh tremble and my blood run icy, it is instead a silhouette, rising, nude from the water. The man is enormous, dwarfing both me and Dagon in mere height alone. He has the most distinctive eyes I've ever seen, which glow, ever brighter in a pale, cold blue as he walks ashore, looking down upon me and Dagon as he approaches.

"Please... please... don't hurt him," I beg, feeling weak, meek, and useless.

"I don't want to hurt you. Step away from the demon." He growls this warning, no mercy in his stare as mahogany tousled locks drip down onto his ripped pectorals. His arm is tattooed, something I had thought reserved only for criminals or barbarians, and I try my hardest not to linger on the other aspects of him which could make me stare for longer than I might admit as a woman of status.

"He's not a demon!" I explain, placing his head in my lap and cradling him as the dark locks of his hair fall across the satin of my skirt. His face is pale and his eyes dull, horrifying me more than any other time I've laid eyes upon his face.

"What do you know about it? Get out of the way!" Something glints in the light as the hunter speaks, his eyes burning feral in the darkness and his muscles bulging, dripping wet. I turn to see that in his hand he's holding a long silver spear, unlike anything I've ever seen. It's sleek and futuristic looking, with no hilt or handle, simply carved as one solid piece of metal.

"Please! Don't hurt him!" I plead. The man bends down, gripping me by the shoulders and throwing me aside from his target. A fleeting softness captures the hunter's face at my panic and he speaks to me like I'm a child.

"I know you're frightened, but you don't understand. He's evil. He doesn't have a soul," he expresses and my eyes widen. I am contemplating this for a moment, shocked into paralysis on the sand as the hunter raises the spear over Dagon's slumped form.

He doesn't have a soul. The words echo in my mind, wrong.

As the spear falls through the air in a sudden and unapologetic darting motion, I throw myself forward, not caring for the consequences, not caring for the pain, only caring to protect what I know to be true.

Dagon *does* have a soul, I know he does, and it is just like mine. It is the soul of a poet.

Four

"She was a phantom of delight,
When first she gleamed upon my sight."
Wordsworth- 'She was a Phantom of delight' (1815)

I return to consciousness, unsure of whether I am being brutally tortured as my throat feels as though it is being shredded like wet crepe paper. I strain, trying to move but finding myself lost to sensation.

"She's waking." I hear the sentiment sound in a familiar voice and my heart lifts in my chest, causing me to open my eyes.

"The transformation would have been quicker if I could have gotten her to the white marble chapel near the Occulta Mirum, but I'd say we're a little too far afield for that." The voice of the hunter shocks me as I stare up into icy blue eyes which peer down, no longer filled with cruelty, but with concern.

"Wh... what happened?" I ask, sitting up and taking in my surroundings. My eyesight is made glorious as I lift a hand and find myself naked. I cover myself, immediately afraid, before I catch the silvery reflective lines casting shadows upon my luminous skin.

I am underwater.

Looking down at myself, I find my legs bound in shimmering silver scale, heavy as I try to move, but not more so than the million layers of skirt and bustle I am used to toting around town. My breasts and modesty are maintained by the continual shimmering of flesh to scale, and I raise a hand to my neck, wincing as my fingertips move to caress three parallel slashes either side of my throat.

Gills, I muse, rising effortlessly off the flat bed of rock on which I've been laid for hours, maybe even days.

"You're a natural, Ophelia! Bravo!" The hunter claps, his eyes alight with an excitement all together unexpected.

"You... you stabbed me!" I accuse him, flexing my tailfin from left to right and rising so I am at eye-level with him. I'm shaky in my motion, but finding myself adapting with ease.

This might even be more freeing than walking, I muse.

"I... I did." He looks ashamed of himself, resting a palm on the back of his neck and rubbing it nervously.

"Ophelia, it is alright. You saved me from a terrible fate." Dagon's voice penetrates my rage and I turn to him, seeing him finally fully immersed in the water, where he belongs.

"A terrible misunderstanding," the hunter adds, looking guiltily betwixt us with a frown on his face.

"I.... I don't understand. I'm... a mermaid?" I query, shocked beyond what I ever thought possible. I thought this was myth, carved from the exquisite words of Hans Christian Andersen.

"Yes. You have been chosen, blessed by Atargatis, our goddess, beloved of Poseidon. Chosen," the hunter explains and my mind continues to race, like a champion race horse held back for far too long.

"Excuse me, but who are you?" I enquire of the hunter, his face more genteel than I ever would have imagined last night. As my mind moves back to his blue irises, shining out from the darkness, I look upward, to where the frothing waves separate me from the now risen sun.

"My name is Orion." The merman introduces himself, distracting me from the sunlight as I move to take in his form, still moving from left to right in the water, practicing using the new and powerful muscles with which I am now endowed. He is covered in royal blue scales, which extend from his waist down into a fin longer and grander than my own. His eyes are startling in their contrast to that which I now notice is a scale eye mask surrounding his brow and falling in a spattering across the bridge of his nose.

"I'm Ophelia, but I'm sure Dagon already told you that," I reply, my heart racing in my chest as I take in everything which is changing so utterly in but moments.

"Yes, he did. I think... I think you might be his soulmate," Orion announces and the look on Dagon's face turns from concerned to surprised, hopeful even, as the gold of his gaze brightens within the murk of the water. My hair swills around me, moving, stiffer than usual but remarkably longer than I remember as it has fallen out of my usual up-do. I reach up to my face as I blush at the term, which means so much, and yet is still so unclear in definition, finding my own eyes surrounded by scales, too.

"What does that mean exactly?" I ask, looking to Dagon and feeling my eyes widen as I take him in fully. His body is clothed only in threadbare trousers, and his hair floats around him in a seaweed-esque slick as his gills open and close rapidly on either side of his throat.

"When Atargatis created the mer, she bound each one of us with a maiden, created from part of our soul. It is to make the eternal service to her easier on us," he explains, and I nod slowly, hanging on each word desperately as if were a poet.

"It cannot be. I am not a mer. I am not blessed. I am cursed." Dagon's eyes fall to the floor, ashamed as the map of green scales cast dark shadows across his profile. I frown, still not understanding.

"So... I'm not bound to him?" I query Orion, watching as he, too, frowns, seemingly unsure of his words in expression but trying to sound definitive in intent.

"I have never yet met a mortal so willing to fall upon a monster's chest and sacrifice herself for no good reason. I believe you are a gift to him. He tells me Poseidon cursed him because he freed Atargatis from her mermaid prison, but the other side of this story is that maybe Atargatis wanted to be freed. Perhaps Ophelia is her way of thanking you for resolving her time on earth and returning her to the heavens." He gives us the explanation and Dagon moves over to me in the water, his legs manoeuvring the current only too naturally - frog-like almost.

"I would not be so bold as to assume that is true. Only your deepest known truth, your own soul, can tell you whether we are destined." Dagon almost pleads with his gaze, willing me to be his, willing me to end his eternal solitude, and yet I feel terrified at the prospect of loving someone. I barely know how to love myself.

"I feel like I know you... I feel drawn to you. I will not deny it. But I am afraid. I have awakened a new being entirely. I know not even what I am," I express and the fire behind his eyes does not diminish, but rather tames itself into a hearty burn, hope still alive within him at the prospect of my company.

"I accept your reservations, this is far from a normal situation." He nods to me, placing a scaled, velvet-textured palm on my shoulder. His touch sends a warmth flooding through me and I wonder if in fact I really am made for him. It is too soon to tell, and yet I cannot help but feel inclined to agree with the explanation of Orion the hunter already.

"Come, Ophelia, we should exercise your new muscles before they atrophy." Orion takes my hand, leading me forward as Dagon watches us, jealousy flying across his face as we move through the water, past the shallow drop-off where I've awakened and into deeper water.

I practice diving, making my way effortlessly through the liquid and breathing it as though it were air. Orion holds my hand, guiding me and staring at me with pity in his eyes after a few minutes.

"What?" I ask, unable to stop a grin from spreading across my lips, enjoying real freedom for perhaps the first time in my life.

"I'm sorry I... well, killed you," he apologises, and I feel myself begin to laugh uncontrollably, the mirth stemming deep from within my sternum.

"I understand... I suppose it's easy to judge based on appearance. I thought you were terrifying," I admit, and he laughs.

"I shouldn't have assumed he was a demon. I suppose if I'd have asked you then you would have thought me one," he expresses, and I nod.

"I would have." I twirl in the water, spinning and watching my arms move with my momentum, glowing against the grey-green of the gloomy Atlantic waters.

"I see how you look at him. I believe it is destiny that you were turned beneath the full moon. Life is funny that way." He adds the sentiment as though he wants to dull the sting of my death. Oddly enough, as I rise through the water toward the surface, I find myself lacking a care for the departure of my mortality. I am free of expectation, free of fear - for now at least - and am immersed in the natural world in a way I have always dreamed of, and yet never believed would be possible for a woman, let alone myself.

"I know not what will happen between us now. I would not be so bold as to assume." I smile at him, as though to infer that I am quite content to court with Dagon, despite the fact that others may turn from his form. I look at him, watching us in the water from afar, and feel my heart flutter, the kind of feeling that only the words of dead men have ever stirred before.

"Careful not to break the surface, Ophelia. The sun is lethal to you now," Orion warns and I still in my ascent toward the frothy surface, confused.

"But I am immortal, am I not?" I ask him, wondering if this is in fact true. Dagon's immortal life was a punishment, but I assume the mermen and mermaids of Atargatis are also of this breed, especially seeing as Orion has previously listed this as a reason for soulmates.

"Yes, to an extent, you will live forever, but you can be killed. The sun will do it swiftly. You can only go ashore by the three nights of the full moon," he explains, and I nod, twisting my arm over my head and pirouetting, feeling for the first time in my life, like dancing.

"Do you have a soulmate, Orion?" I ask him, wondering if I might query him about the nature of his feelings toward her so as to ascertain the exact nature of my connection with Dagon.

"I do not. Though, I have been waiting so long now I can only hope that she finds me quickly. Days on the sea are lonely, as I'm sure Dagon will attest to," he replies, looking devastated as he circles me, and I twirl once more in the water. As I am mid spin, I find myself caught in the velvety caress of Dagon's embrace.

"Hello," I say, surprised by his sudden presence as his arm curls around my waist and he holds his body stiffly apart from mine, respecting the proper boundaries to which I have become so accustomed.

"She was a phantom of delight, when first she gleamed upon my sight." Dagon recites the words of the poet we both love so much, as we dance in the water, moving up and down in height as well as round in cyclical pathways through the seemingly infinite depths of the water.

"I am glowing," I observe, raising my hand from his forearm where it is resting as I practice my backwards stroke, waltzing with him as though I've known him for years. Our motions are matched exactly, as though we were made for one another.

I catch Orion watching us from afar, but pay him little attention as Dagon's gaze catches my own in its irregular charms.

As I stare into his eyes, the gateways to his oh so present soul, I no longer see the plague of scales marring his flesh, or the scars which scatter the length and width of his face. I instead see a man, a man with whom I have so very much in common, despite the fact I barely know him.

"I feel as though I know you," I whisper, my voice breaking and my heart pounding, heavy and cumbersome beneath my scaled breast.

"Maybe you don't know me in person, not yet, but perhaps in reading the romantics, in knowing the minds of those who are invested in substance, we are both... very much compatible." His words are sweet, and he leans in, his soft and wide lips grazing my cheek as he kisses me, and I flush, replying as a flurry of future imaginings, of romantic dreams I did not know belonged to me realised.

"I, for one, could not agree more."

BETTY

As I sit, tucking into my breakfast, I watch the ticking clock opposite the dining room table, readying to call the police once again to enquire about the case of my missing niece, Darling Ophelia. Her mother is asleep upstairs, devastated and exhausted from crying, and I cannot help but feel this is somewhat my fault. I should have kept a closer eye on her, been more diligent, and yet I cannot regret giving her the freedom I have, not really, for we as women now, have so little choice past the age of marriage, and I have always believed that youth should be cherished and enjoyed.

"Mrs. Lovecraft. A letter for you," Albert announces, bringing a thick envelope through from the hallway and passing it to me over my steaming breakfast tea and increasingly soggy, unfortunately neglected crumpets. I have had little appetite, unsurprisingly, in the last week, ever since Ophelia has not come home.

Turning the parchment over in my hands, I feel my thinning, wrinkled flesh tremble at the finery of the paper. It seems important, and the wax seal bears the symbol of a trident, something I've never seen before. Opening the envelope swiftly, I pull out a long, folded piece of waxy parchment and my eyes bulge as I read the address.

Dearest Aunt,

I am writing to you under the most wonderful, and yet most peculiar set of circumstances which one could possibly imagine. I have met a man, well, almost a man, but not quite, who goes by the name of Dagon. I have found my destiny with him, and have found myself quite taken from you all by the sea.

You must not worry, Aunt, and you must take care of my sisters and my mother. I could have written to them, but I feel strongly that this story would not have been received with the open-mindedness it requires.

I have been blessed, you see, by the sea Goddess, Atargatis, and given new life, eternal and everlasting beneath the waves. My soul has been crafted to match that of another, a man cursed by Poseidon with a monstrous plague upon his flesh, but this has not stopped me from falling very much smitten with what lies beneath the shallows of his appearance. For it is beneath the aesthetics which our society so much relies on as a crutch to represent what is good and what is right, through what looks a certain way, that I have found riches in him, precious substance for which I have always so craved. He is a darling man, sweet and tender in our courtship, and yet he continually pleads that he is not worthy of my youth, of my beauty. He has taken the words of the sea God, Poseidon, who is seemingly unforgiving in even the most genteel of lights, very much into his heart, and for this I feel I must take action. We are heading across the ocean, searching for a cure to his ailment, a way for him to be restored to what he once was.

We do not know what lies ahead, nor can we ever know what the Gods and Goddesses have in store for us, but I wish you could see that which surrounds me now. The luxurious generosity of the mer who ended my life, or should I say birthed me into the life which I truly belong, is truly astounding. Here I have no rules, no expectations thrust upon me. I am myself, utterly and in no restrained form, finding what I believe to be love with no bustle, no corset, no hat, only me and my mind, my heart, and soul.

Please do not mourn for me, for I am more alive than I have ever been, and I am where I belong. I could not have beared the torment of being married for a dowry, or used as a brood mare and left to wither. My life has turned into the story I have always wished to read, and been filled with the substance I have always craved.

I hope you and Uncle Howard treat each other well, find contentedness. Perhaps you could tell him this story and he will find the substance in it to sculpt the marble of his writer's block into a statue worthy of both your vibrant spirits.

All my love,

Your Ophelia.

I gape at the paper for more than a moment, blinking as Albert watches me with a queer glance. I know I cannot show this to her mother, nor her sisters, for they will think me mad. Yet I cannot deny that this story doesn't seem beyond the realms of possibility. The Greek myths must have come from somewhere… so perhaps this really is all true.

I sit in silence at the breakfast table until my tea is gone cold and the butter of my crumpets has sept through to the fine china of my plate. I ponder what to do, re-reading the letter over and over, before taking decisive action and asking Albert to bring me a fountain pen and parchment.

He scurries through from the study, silver tray in hand, as I clear the remnants of my stony breakfast and take the writing instrument from him, wielding the pen as the most powerful weapon at my disposal.

I inhale, sure of my decision to share the story, but only once, writing as fast as I can muster… and begin…

To Mr. Howard Phillips Lovecraft…

Epilogue

ATARGATIS
ELYSIUM SHORES- THE HIGHER PLAINS

"You did what!?" Poseidon's face contorts in fury, his eyes sparking white through with forks of lightning as he launches off the bedcloud and turns on me, arms throbbing with veins which look like they might burst forth from beneath his skin and throttle me.

"Poseidon, it is time. He has suffered enough," I protest, feeling my heart slowing as I try to remain calm after his initial outburst.

"You gave him a *soulmate?!* The man who murdered you? The man who lusted after you with his eyes? You gave him the most sacred bond between two souls?" He is breathing so heavily I wonder how I have not yet been pulled toward him with the force of his inhale alone.

"I gave him a soulmate. After all, he saved me. He returned me to you. Didn't you miss me while I was gone?" I flutter my lashes, trying to persuade him to bend, trying to cause him to see my point of view. Instead, though, this only angers him more.

"I do not know how much longer I can abide by you defying me, woman! I am your husband!" he barks, crossing his arms across his chest. I cock an eyebrow, realising that flirting just isn't going to cut it this time.

"And I am your wife! But that doesn't stop you from doing whatever the hell you damn well please and ignoring me, does it now? What about your pet, Solustus? Because I told you it would turn into a total disaster of catastrophic proportions! It didn't stop you making him though, did it?" I am usually the calm to his storm, the tranquillity to his raging tide, but this time I will not break, nor bend. This time I will fight.

The waters below become choppy in the mortal world and the seas crash into the land over and over, receding only as we pause for breath before unleashing the next bout of pain with our tongues.

Perhaps we will never agree. Perhaps we aren't supposed to. Perhaps, in fact, our juxtaposition is the most crucial of cruxes for the world below to stand upon. Perhaps we will never know.

Regardless, the argument and the storm below, much like our eternal love, rages on between us, unstoppable.

THE END

WHAT IS THE KRISTY NICOLLE FANTASY INFINIVERSE?

The Kristy Nicolle Fantasy Infiniverse is a fictional universe with endless possibilities. Spanning up to 70+ novels, shorts and novellas. this work in progress is forging a world where mermaids, demons, angels, dragons, faeries, unicorns, witches, vampires, gods, goddesses and more come together across multiple dimensions shared with you in sagas, series and standalones to collide in the most magical way possible.

The First Saga in The Infiniverse is
THE QUEENS OF FANTASY SAGA which consists of
THE TIDAL KISS TRILOGY
THE ASHEN TOUCH TRILOGY
THE AETHERIAL EMBRACE TRILOGY
keep up to date with the infiniverse that just keeps on growing at
WWW.KRISTYNICOLLE.COM

QUEENS OF *Fantasy*
A TIDAL KISS SHORT

ABOUT THE QUEENS OF FANTASY SAGA

Kristy Nicolle's Queens of Fantasy Saga is a collection of 3 trilogies, following the lives of three extraordinary women and their journeys, both personal and fantastical, into three unique but interconnected fantasy worlds. The first trilogy in the saga, 'The Tidal Kiss Trilogy', captures the fantastical underwater world of the Occulta Mirum and its scaly tailed residents as their world, which seemed stable for so long, begins to shift.

Want more Tidal Kiss Trilogy magic?

BOOKS IN THIS TRILOGY
The Kiss That Killed Me
The Kiss That Saved Me
The Kiss That Changed Me

Follow the Trilogy @
Website: www.kristynicolle.com
Facebook: https://www.facebook.com/authorkristynicolle
Twitter: Nicolle_Kristy
Instagram: authorkristynicolle
Goodreads: Search The Tidal Kiss Trilogy
Photographs by the fabulously talented Trish Thompson

THE TIDAL KISS TRILOGY:

The Kiss That Killed Me
The Kiss That Saved Me
The Kiss That Changed Me

TIDAL KISS NOVELLAS

Vexed
The Tank

TIDAL KISS SHORTS

Waiting For Gideon
Beyond The Shallows

OTHER QUEENS OF FANTASY TRILOGIES:

THE ASHEN TOUCH TRILOGY

The Opal Blade
The Onyx Hourglass
The Obsidian Shard

THE AETHERIAL EMBRACE TRILOGY

Indigo Dusk
Violet Dawn
Lavender Storm

FOR PREDICTED RELEASE DATES VISIT
WWW.KRISTYNICOLLE.COM

Printed in Poland
by Amazon Fulfillment
Poland Sp. z o.o., Wrocław